T0131997

THE OLD POND SLUMS

Daniel Silverhawk

• Special thanks to Sarah W. and Ryan M. for their support in the publication of this series without whom this series would not be made available for your enjoyment.

• stevensgreetingsinc@yahoo.com

To order additional copies of this book, contact:
Xlibris
1-888-795-4274
www.Xlibris.com
Orders@Xlibris.com

THE OLD POND SLUMS

Daniel Silverhawk

Once upon a time in the old pond slums
Lived a most talkative toad always chomping his gums
He talked about everything he learned in his life
He talked about his tadpoles and his fine warted wife

He talked about the birds
that flew over head

He talked about the fish that go swimming instead

He added his thoughts making his stories seem real
then he filled in the gaps with words of great skill.
He spoke of so many things he never had seen
but the way that he spoke made him seem very keen.

He talked night and day without taking a rest
He spoke without fear of being put to the test.

He continued to speak his gums chomping away
with whatever the flavor he had chosen that day.
Wintergreen or spearmint or bright cinnamon red
gumming up all his stories with the words that he said

As long as the taste would stay fresh in his cheeks
his long rolling tongue formed the message he speaks.
He chose his words carefully to express the best theme
like choosing his gum for a flavor extreme

Every story was different but they were all just the same;
stories of the future and from where we all came.
He chomped and he chomped with all that he had
he chomped with authority from his grand lily pad.

Like the king of the pond with a crown full of jewels
the most talkative toad could recite all the rules
He remembered the stories he told long ago
which he would never repeat unless a frog had to know

He spoke of the deep things from deep in his throat
he chomped on them lightly and their aroma did float.
Just a bubble of babbling rising up from his thoughts
changing fiction to action and calling the shots

Then came the day when his final words he had spoke
the most talkative toad did suddenly croak
All the frogs gathered together to say their goodbyes
but none of them spoke to no big surprise

The talkative toad would know just what to say
but when silence was heard the words went away.
It was so sad in the pond slums everything seemed to stop
the pond was so quiet you could hear a drip drop.

They buried the old toad along with his gums
there was not a sound heard in all the pond slums
except for the chirping of the crickets was heard
making lots of strange noises without saying a word

Then one little froggie so tiny and brave
popped a bubblegum bubble in the pond near the grave.
The exciting new flavor drew a fairly large crowd
the smallest frog willing to share his expressions out loud
he started asking questions why everyone was so sad
from the tops of his lungs from the grand lily pad

He reminded the toads of their family and friends
he reminded the frogs of a memory that mends
he encouraged the frogs to talk to their peers
and requested the toads relieve their worst fears
He chomped and he pleaded until the toads understood
that what he was saying was for everyone's good

Then all the frogs started chomping at the same time,
filling the pond full of ribbets because ribbets all rhyme.
The pond was soon hopping and leaping about
thanks to one tiny froggie with the guts to speak out.
And that's how all the frogs in all the pond slums
started croaking all night and chomping their gums

They like to blow bubbles and show off their long tongue
they hop to attention when it comes to their young
The water is their safety though they prefer the dry land
they relax on their lily pads and from there take a stand.

So to all the little tadpoles that are finding their feet
stand up and be counted don't be afraid to compete
There are many ponds out there that resemble these slums,
ponds that are quiet and in need of your gums
So the next time you find yourself in the slums of the pond
with the tadpoles and frogs and the toads you can bond

The beginning...

Printed in the United States
By Bookmasters